A Hotshot Christmas

a Firehawks Hotshot romance story
by
M. L. Buchman

Buchman Bookworks

Other works by M.L. Buchman

Flash of Fire
Wild Fire

SMOKEJUMPERS
Wildfire at Dawn
Wildfire at Larch Creek
Wildfire on the Skagit

<u>Delta Force</u>
Target Engaged
Heart Strike

<u>Angelo's Hearth</u>
Where Dreams are Born
Where Dreams Reside
Maria's Christmas Table
Where Dreams Unfold
Where Dreams Are Written

<u>Eagle Cove</u>
Return to Eagle Cove
Recipe for Eagle Cove
Longing for Eagle Cove
Keepsake for Eagle Cove

<u>Deities Anonymous</u>
Cookbook from Hell: Reheated
Saviors 101

<u>Dead Chef Thrillers</u>
Swap Out!
One Chef!
Two Chef!

<u>SF/F Titles</u>

Nara
Monk's Maze
The Me and Elsie Chronicles

Get a free Starter Library at:
www.mlbuchman.com

1

Sheila inspected the heavy dark beams and white plaster of the restaurant. A hostess—in a bad Bavarian costume of ruffled sleeves, low-cut above blousy, cotton-cupped breasts—smiled at her as she sashayed across the hardwood floor in incongruous heels.

"Table for one?" Just one notch too perky for her to swallow.

"No, thanks. Just looking in." Sheila turned abruptly and nearly trampled a couple and their kids coming in the door.

Civilians!

Too close!

She kept the epithet to herself and stepped around them and back out into the crisp darkness.

To her left was the snow sprinkled faux-Bavarian town of Leavenworth, Washington, so perfect it was like a goddamn life-sized snow globe. To her right was a McDonald's with a wood and plaster Germanic facade. She'd promised herself that she'd do better than McD's for a Thanksgiving Day dinner, but crowds were kind of a problem for her and the town was packed.

Saddle up, girl.

She didn't even bother raising her camo jacket's collar as she turned to tromp through the snow—even the damned falling snow was picturesque—and into the heart of the town. Somewhere there had to be a bar with a burger, a brew, and a minimum of Bavarian.

She'd been driving to...well, nowhere. She'd been driving *away* from the family Thanksgiving in Seattle. Five hours through packed city roads and over slick mountain ones.

Not a soul understood what it meant that she was out of the Army. No one got that a TBI diagnosis didn't mean she was nuts. Traumatic Brain Injury meant that she'd been blown up one too many times for the Army to trust her at the wheel of her big transport truck. Didn't meant she was crazy. Please let it not mean she was crazy.

Which totally explained why she was in a resort town, that looked about as inauthentic as most of the ones in the real Bavaria did, looking for a quiet place to get drunk on Thanksgiving night.

A polka band playing out on the town's square made her wonder how the tuba player's lips didn't freeze to his mouthpiece. Children skidded around despite all the salt and sand laid down on the sidewalks. One ran into her legs hard enough to fall back on its butt.

She stopped, knelt down, and picked up the kid to put it back on its feet. *See, acting perfectly normal. Helping out.*

It took one look at her, burst out crying, and raced away.

Sheila closed her eyes for a moment… before standing and continuing through town. She crossed the street to get clear of the square.

Bavarian Bistro. Not a chance.

Soup Cellar. *O Tannenbaum* playing on the juke because Thanksgiving was over in another half dozen hours. She didn't even make it halfway down the stairs.

She closed her eyes to get past the garish Christmas store and let the tourists bounce off her until she was clear.

King Ludwig's. The Mad King. Not a freaking chance.

She jostled and was nudged along until she fell out the other end of the town. Four blocks. She'd survived four blocks. *Sometimes the victories are small.* She hated when the psychs were right, especially when it felt more like defeat.

At the far end of the tourist strip, the town collapsed back into small American town. Dimly lit, cold. She leaned against the concrete wall of a closed warehouse and did what she could to catch her breath.

"Been following you," a deep male voice.

She really didn't need this shit right now. She rested her hand on her sidearm, but the Glock 19 wasn't on her hip where it should be. Where it *used* to be.

"No need for that," the voice continued

as she started a hand up to her concealed shoulder carry. Her back was turned, he shouldn't have been able to spot her motion.

Sheila risked a glance.

Big guy. Ten feet back. Standing planted on the sidewalk. No one behind or to the sides. Alone. She recognized the stance.

"You got somewhere to be?" His voice was soft, steady. She could deal with that. "I can help you get there."

Sheila could only shake her head. No, she had nowhere to be. Might never again.

He waited a while before continuing, like he was studying her and thinking.

"What?"

"Got a place you might like."

"Shit! Not looking for a goddamn roll in the hay."

"More like snow, this time of year," he said it with barely a hint of smile. "Besides, it's not that kinda place. And my wife would kick my ass."

"Must be some tough wife to keep you on a short leash."

He shrugged, "Works for me."

Sheila stared at him, but he just waited.

Military recognized military. She could do worse. She offered him a shrug. Didn't really matter anyway.

He pointed past her.

She waved for him to lead the way.

Being a smart man, he also saw that he should circle wide out onto the empty street rather than try to come by her on the sidewalk.

2

Randall sat close beside Jess and Jill. They were about the funniest damn couple on the whole team and who better to sit with while Thanksgiving dinner was cooking.

The two Js met on a wildfire in the middle of last season and Jess had somehow swept her up before she'd even hit the damned fire line.

Or maybe she'd swept him up. Randall had long since learned that being five-four, blond, and cute as hell had nothing to do with Jill's skills. The woman totally rocked it, offering her sunny smile the whole time.

"Sure you don't have a twin sister?" He asked for the hundredth time.

"Nope! My moms only had the one kid."

"Crap!" They shared a smile. He'd met her moms at the wedding, two of Seattle's finest firefighters.

A cold gust of air crawled up his back.

"Close the goddamn door!" Randall shivered. He really should move, but this crew area of the Leavenworth fire station was maxed out. The volunteer firefighters and their families would have made it crowded enough. But Captain Cantrell had invited his daughter's entire Interagency Hotshot Crew to his Thanksgiving Feed. No wildfires in the winter in the Cascade Mountains, but half of them had found ways to keep busy and keep local. Candace was the kind of superintendent who helped make good things like that happen.

"Happy Thanksgiving to you too, asshole," Luke smacked him on top of the head as he came through the door and they both laughed.

Then a shadow slipped in behind him and did close the door. She was close to six feet, not gaunt, but not far from it. She had dark hair that fell in soft waves past her shoulders and narrowed her pale face even more. Her fists were jammed deep in the pockets of her unzipped hunting jacket. She wore a turtleneck and a thin white sweater that flowed down her slender frame, apparently oblivious to the biting cold.

She wasn't exactly beautiful, but she was as dramatic as hell.

"What's your problem?" Her voice was low, rough.

"Breathing around you," was all Randall managed.

Somewhere in the background Jill laughed. He couldn't tell whether or not it was at him, but he sure wasn't going to risk looking away to find out. She might evaporate if he did, or stab him.

Her dark eyes studied him for a long moment, then glanced aside to look out the door's frosted window.

"Sorry. Rude. I know. Never think first. You'll have to get used to that if you're going to hang around me. I'm Randall. Randall Jones," he held out a hand.

Again those piercing eyes studied

him for a long moment. Then she cursed emphatically.

He started to draw back his hand, but she reached out and shook it once. Solidly. With a damned strong grip. And her fingers were cold as ice.

"Sorry. I'm having trouble around people at the moment."

"Oh, then you're fine here. No people at all. Only firefighters and a couple folks stupid enough to marry them." *And you're babbling, dude. Rein it in.*

"Okay," and the ghost actually smiled—a thin one, but definitely there. It looked amazing on her. "As long as there aren't any actual people."

"Scout's honor," he did his best Boy Scout three-fingered salute.

She snapped upright and was most of the way to a hard salute before she froze, went momentarily wide-eyed, then rammed her fist back into her pocket hard enough that he was surprised she didn't punch through the fabric.

"Sorry," he didn't know what else to say. "I'm…" Maybe it would be better if he just introduced her around or… "Are you hungry? We can go see if it's done cooking." Even though he could see by the long table that the turkeys weren't out yet.

She studied him again, then glanced sideways at Luke.

Randall hadn't even noticed that he was still there, watching them.

Luke gave a shrug to her as if to say, "Up to you."

Sheila turned back to him. Again that long pause before she spoke, as if she had to practice it in her head first before speaking.

"Food would be okay," she finally managed. "A beer sure wouldn't hurt."

Searching for a possible path through the crowd, and seeing the way his ghost was still hanging close to the door, he decided for expediency. He grabbed his jacket off the back of his chair.

"It's quieter that way," he pointed out the door.

Again, her first look went to Luke, who nodded that it would be okay.

He held the door for her and led her outside.

3

Randall's grip had been strong, solid. What Sheila would expect from a firefighter.

"Were you a SEAL too? Like Luke." He asked as he led her toward the back of the building. It was dark except for the distant lights of the town reflecting off the snow, but the path was shoveled. She could smell the thick pine of the trees growing close behind the station.

He didn't move like a trained hand-to-hand fighter. She'd wager she could take him down if necessary, even without her sidearm.

Shoulder carry, not hip. She still needed to change that habit.

"He's a SEAL?" That fit. The silence and the arrogant level of self-assuredness. An unarmed man who simply said, "No need for that," as she'd prepared to draw on him. SEAL? Unarmed? Not likely. "No. Not like Luke. There aren't any SEAL women. I was in the Army. A HEMTT driver."

"A what?"

"Big trucks. A Heavy Expanded Mobility Tactical Truck. Also just called a 'heavy.' I carried anything lighter than an Abrams tank." That shut up most men.

"Did you like it?"

Not Randall. He continued on cheerfully as if they were having an actual conversation and it was okay that she'd driven a massive Army transport for a living…until she couldn't anymore.

He held open a door for her at the rear of the building and she saw that they were entering the back of an equipment bay. A line of shining fire trucks and a pair of polished ambulances were lined up in a neat row. At the far end, one of the doors was rolled halfway up and she could see some guys standing around a big closed-top grill nosed just outside the open door. No crowd pressure in the vast bay which was a good thing. By their feet was a cooler and most of them were nursing a beer. *Target acquired.*

"Yeah," she looked at the beautiful rigs all lined up. "I liked it a lot." Maybe too pretty for her taste. She preferred a machine built to get down and dirty, but the ladder truck could definitely tempt her.

He led her up to the group.

"Captain Cantrell," he began introducing her around. "And Candace is the super on our IHC team."

Father-daughter. Obvious right down to how they stood—sure of themselves but without any real ego display.

"You met her husband Luke."

Which explained just who could keep a SEAL on that short leash.

"And this is Patsy, one of our two foremen. Her husband's the town baker and is around somewhere."

Again, a solid grip and a questioning eye. IHC. Interagency Hotshot Crew. That meant that Randall wasn't just some firefighter. He walked into the wilderness to fight wildfires with a chainsaw and an axe—a very real form of hand-to-hand combat. She suspected it took some serious balls despite his easygoing manner. It also meant "team," which explained the outsider looks she was getting. They were being nice about it though, so she tamped down any need to get out. Especially when "out" would mean going back among the flocks of happy tourists. Families. Candace handed her a beer from the cooler so she'd definitely stick for a bit.

"And I still don't know your name. Sorry." Firefighter Randall Jones was a guy who couldn't stop apologizing. Very strange.

"Sheila Williams."

"And this is Sheila," he introduced her to everyone else.

He didn't mention the Army, which she appreciated. But he did mouth her name a few times to himself to make sure he had it down. Which was kind of cute.

4

Randall shadowed her the whole evening. At first because he wanted to, but later she seemed to appreciate it. She didn't exactly open up, but she did appear to relax. When a plate was offered piled high with grilled turkey and all the fixings, she took it. When he pointed to the fire station donation box and told her they were all kicking in a ten, she slipped in a twenty.

Luke floated by on occasion, but made no big deal of it. He'd expected to lose her to Luke, some form of ex-military bonding, but Sheila didn't seem inclined to leave his side which worked fine for him. Even if it was just for the evening, it was nice to have a date. Of sorts. Eventually she told him the story of the Seattle family dinner she'd bugged out of. He couldn't get her to laugh, but he raised that soft smile a couple of times and called it good.

Sheila hung around right through the cleanup chores, earning her a round of thanks that she did her best to shrug off.

"Where are you staying? I'll walk you there."

She shrugged, "Gotta find a room. And I know how to walk myself just fine."

"Won't find one on a Thanksgiving in Leavenworth." Randall glanced at Luke who seemed to be making a point of not watching them. "I've got a couch. Not much of a place, but you're welcome to it."

She didn't do that sideways check-in with Luke that had punctuated so much of the evening. Instead she looked at him carefully. "Just the couch."

His nod of agreement settled it, at least until they were headed to his place through the cold night air. It was late enough that all of the tourists had gone to bed. He liked the town at these times—still all bedazzled up, but only the occasional local walking by with a friendly nod and a "Hey."

"No luggage?"

She swung open her still unzipped coat, fists again in pockets. "Left in a bit of a hurry." By the sound of her family dinner, he would have too.

"I can lend you a t-shirt, maybe scrounge some shorts," he unlocked the door to his apartment and led her up the stairs. And did his best not to picture how she'd look in them.

5

The result was far more incredible than he'd imagined. Her narrow shoulders made his "Firefighters Bring the Heat" ride low and expose a lot of neck and collar. Even though it was his longest one, it rode barely past her hips. A pair of gym shorts revealed long, powerful legs.

He did his best to hide his astonishment with a cough and knew he'd completely failed. He enjoyed strong competent women…if he didn't, he was on the wrong crew. Candace had drawn more than the standard share of women to her team—one or two women was still the exception on a twenty-person IHC, and they had five. But not a one was like the dark-haired soldier standing in the middle of his small living room.

"You want to do it, I don't mind."

"Want to?" He gasped it out on a half laugh. How could a man *not* want to; she was stunning. Randall didn't know what self control had him walking up to her, placing his hands on her shoulders, and looking her right in the eyes. "Let me know when *you* want to. Then we'll talk."

He waited for that odd processing lag that she had. Finally she just nodded and turned for the couch. He got out of there before she bent over to adjust the blanket and made the t-shirt ride up higher than it already did. Besides, he'd seen the size of the handgun she'd slipped under her pillow.

6

Sheila stayed on the couch that first night and puzzled at Randall's comment. What did *she* want? There was the thousand-dollar question.

The door to what she wanted had been closed. The Army offered to let her stay in if she would drive domestic, but no foreign action. She'd told them just how far out of the daylight they could ram it. Their ever-so knowing and tolerant smiles—they'd all read her psych profile after all—almost earned them a personal demonstration. The black ops contractors didn't need drivers, they needed operators—she'd checked. As far as "want" went, she hadn't looked any further than that.

Three more days and nights with Randall didn't add a lot of clarity. During the days they went on long cold hikes through the crisp mountain air. In the evenings, they'd sometimes meet up with a few of the others in a locals' bar—the kind of place she'd been trying to find that first night—or they'd end up back at his apartment playing backgammon or watching some action flick.

Sunday night, end of the weekend, she went to lie on the couch when the first bit of *want* seeped into her brain. She didn't care about the sex one way or the other, but it would be nice to be held. What's more, it would be nice to be held by Randall. Somehow all the care she had to take to not be offensive to civilians didn't matter around him.

For once not thinking deeply, she turned aside and followed him through his bedroom door. She'd checked out the place the first day, had the layout clear in her head (including all exits), and could walk right to the bed in the pitch dark.

When she slipped under the covers, it

earned her a grunt of surprise, but no more. She lay against him. For a long frozen moment he lay perfectly still unsure what to do next—it was a moment she knew well. He didn't paw at her or jump her, both of which she was ready for; just part of the price.

Instead, he pulled her in and held on tight.

Somehow he knew that this was what she wanted. No, he wasn't some freaking telepath like those damned Army psychs thought they were. Randall waited while she figured out what she wanted. For a long time, it was exactly what he was giving her.

When she decided it was more, he seemed pretty okay with that as well.

7

Randall knew he was dreaming, but four weeks hadn't been enough to wake him up so far and he was starting to hope it never would. Just as she had that first night, Sheila had started on the periphery, staying in town when he went to work on the Monday after Thanksgiving. That had lasted her active nature about two days.

By the end of the week she had fully integrated into the small business that he and Patsy had set up with Jess and Jill. WUI Cleaners—the name made them laugh even if no one else seemed to get the joke. They specialized in cleaning up the Wildland-Urban Interface around homes, securing them as well as possible against the dangers of wildfire. They dropped dead trees, or ones too close to a house. Around homes pushed into thickly wooded areas, they trimmed off all of the dead lower branches that could act as ladder fuels to take a fire from ground to crown. They'd recently expanded from burn piles into prescribed burns, clearing brush and deadwood from the forest floor with carefully controlled small fires.

Sheila—still oblivious to the cold—started out dragging branches and tending burn piles. It wasn't long before she picked up saw work and finally harness work climbing in the trees. The general lack of snow let them keep busy in Leavenworth, only occasionally shifting down the dry eastern slopes of the Cascades to Cashmere or Wenatchee.

She didn't really open up around the others, but her hesitations shortened over time. They'd talked about the whole TBI thing, looked up the symptoms together, and it didn't quite fit.

"As you just demonstrated, it's not that you

think any slower than I do," Randall observed one night as they lay exhausted together. A good work day around the Kitchner farm, followed by an equally thorough workout with only a short break for delivery pizza in bed. Slow thinking was one of the main signs of a traumatic brain injury and Sheila had shifted over the month from an active lover to an immensely creative one. Combined with her magnificent body, he was a complete goner.

Her silence was her usual answer but he could feel her listening. She was like that when they were making love as well, completely silent but gloriously present.

"It's more like we're all speaking a foreign language and you need time to translate it."

She buried her face against his shoulder for a while before finally responding, "God, I hope you're right. It feels that way. Even as familiar as you feel, there's a strangeness I can't seem to get around."

"Familiar, huh?"

8

Sheila could hear the tease, but she could feel the pain.

Randall felt so much more than "familiar" but she didn't know how to say it. He had welcomed her into his world with no questions asked. A dinner, his couch, his bed, his job, his life.

And what had she offered in return? Her body. There should be more than that.

She considered using it to demonstrate quite how much more than familiar he felt. But it wasn't that simple or that crass...because it *was* more than that.

"You feel…"

And he waited while she searched for the word. It wasn't that sluggish feeling she'd felt back when the Army was giving her the medical discharge. It wasn't even the foreignness issue, though that was the best explanation she'd heard of it.

"I feel…" That was the real problem. Her feelings—other than anger at what had happened, at the raghead who'd blown up her truck, with her inability to say what she meant—were distant, almost vague. She didn't know what she felt and had no idea how to put words to that.

So, she fell back on showing it with her body. But it wasn't merely great sex this time. It was more. It was deeper. She groaned aloud as the layers of defense broke loose inside her. Randall eased his way past more than the barricades of the flesh, he also shattered the massive walls she'd built around her own emotions without realizing.

This time, as her body shuddered with pleasure, it wasn't a release. It was a cleansing.

9

The fire hit and it hit hard. December had been unseasonably dry, less than a foot of snow and a series of warm afternoons that had melted what little fell. The town had brought in snowmaking machines so that they could have a white Christmas.

Patsy's call wrenched them out of deep sleep. Just breaking dawn outside the window.

"We're activated. Move!" And she was gone. Hotshot teams were never mobilized in mid-winter.

He punched Tori's number, remembered that she was wintering with her famous writer husband in Seattle, mumbled an apology for waking her, and hung up. Next on his leg of the phone tree…nobody who was still in town.

Time to move.

He was pulling on his cotton long johns as Sheila stripped off her t-shirt and began doing the same.

"What are you doing?" Other than escalating the hell out of his pulse rate. Not in a hundred years could he get used to the look of her.

"There's a fire." No hesitation at all. No question either.

"You're not…"

He stopped when he saw her baleful gaze.

…a firefighter.

Though he'd trained her in all he could and she'd learned fast, she wasn't trained for wildfire—didn't have her Incident Qualification System "red card." However, he'd long since learned that changing Sheila Williams' mind once she set it was not something that mortal men should attempt. There was no hesitation when she was in work mode. The same thing had happened when they were working for WUI Cleaners. When there was action, Sheila didn't pause for a microsecond. No more wrong with her brain than her stunning body.

Fine. Let Candace try to face her down about the "official" certification.

He watched her pulling on the Nomex fire retardant gear he'd given her as a gift when she'd proved she was going to stick with WUI for a while. A powerful woman climbing into firefighting gear. And not just any woman, but Sheila Williams.

Randall knew what he wanted to see for the rest of his days, and he was looking right at it.

"You're still naked," she said without looking up from lacing her boots.

"Shit!" He finished dressing at firefighter speed.

When they arrived at the station, Candace took one look at Sheila and growled, "I don't have time to argue this shit. Fine. You're attached to Randall's hip. I find you more than ten feet apart, I'm gonna kick your ass off the fire and out of this town."

Then she turned to him, "She dies, it's totally on you." Then she rushed off to ream someone else's ass about something.

"Wipe the surprise off your face, Randall." Sheila gave him a gentle shove to get him into motion. "Let's go."

He led her to the type 3 wildfire engine that hadn't seen a job since October. Built on a truck frame, it carried five people, five hundred gallons of water, and could blast a hundred-and-fifty gallons per minute out of fifteen-hundred feet of hose. The big diesel, rear dualies, and four-wheel drive also meant it could cross over seriously rough terrain.

Sheila went for the driver's door, then stopped with her hand on the handle. "Sorry, old habits." She circled to the passenger side.

Randall had learned that it was easier to just let her drive the work truck, but there were special insurance issues here and he was glad that he didn't have to force it.

Captain Cantrell came by and slapped an address in his hand. "Remote as hell. None of my engines can make it up there. It's up to your team to lead. My men are right behind you."

Randall could see teams of firefighters loading the backs of their four-wheel drive personal vehicles with fire gear and piling aboard. Jess, Candace, and Patsy slid into the back seat of his truck's cab. It was odd having Sheila in Tori's usual seat beside him, not that he was complaining.

Jill actually chirped the tires on the other wildland engine as she pulled out ahead of him along with the rest of the Leavenworth Hotshots wintering in Leavenworth. Ten people. Half their normal crew. They'd need Cantrell's people fast. The problem was that though they were good guys, they were volunteers and would need to be watched like hawks. Along with Sheila…though he'd never found watching her to be a burden.

Together, he and Jill raced the big engines down Highway 2 toward the small town of Dryden.

10

Sheila wasn't ready for the scale of a wildfire or the scale of the change that washed over her easy-going and affable lover. She barely recognized him. Deep in a valley beyond Dryden, a fire was ripping apart the landscape.

"Goddamn winter hunters," his unexpected snarl came from deep in his chest.

"What's wrong with hunters?"

"They're big on exploding targets. Doesn't matter that the damned things are outlawed on state forest land; they love seeing the flash and bang during target practice. Then, if they start a fire, the hunters scram so that they don't get caught and have to pay for the firefight. Not the primary cause of our manmade fires, but it's climbing."

"What are the primaries?"

"Campfires and arsonists. But there aren't any hiking trails back here and arsonists like showier fires than the back hill country. There also hasn't been any lightning lately, which says numbskull hunters. They were probably bored because the elk are staying in the higher pastures due to the mildness of the season." Randall sounded seriously pissed. Army-style pissed, something Sheila didn't know he had in him.

She was already discovering a soft-spot in her head for Randall Jones; this just amped up the developing pile of mush that was her brain. She'd *never* been mushy about a man or anything else before—except maybe her truck before the roadside bomb dismembered it. Actually, she cared more about him than anything before which was a surprise. If you'd asked her a month ago, she'd have said she was past caring about anything ever again.

They swooped off the end of the gravel road they'd been following into the backcountry and the big truck jounced and jostled as he headed into an area that was a combination of meadow and trees. All conifers—mostly scattered—except low in the valley, where the water would accumulate. They made thick clumps down there. Higher on the dry slopes they spread out, and the brown grasses dominated. The fire was climbing both valley walls simultaneously and sending a plume of smoke soaring upward like a line of JDAM bombs. She kept expecting to feel the shock-wave slam into the truck. But the smoke just kept rolling upward in a continuous gray sheet, dark with ash above and bright with flames below.

"Flanks first," Candace called from the back of the truck as Randall slammed it to a halt over two hundred yards away from the fire. Everyone piled out of the back.

"What are they…" Then Sheila stopped asking. Stay in the truck. Watch and learn, just like in the Army.

The firefighters who piled out of the two trucks spread out in a short line. In moments they were swinging their Pulaski fire axes, digging a line across the meadow. Great clumps of grass and dirt were peeled up. They moved in a fast, coordinated action.

The townie firefighters drove up and were soon put to the same task with varying degrees of effectiveness. Just like a fresh shipment of boot camp privates arriving on the line, the main thing they did was make it really clear how skilled the hotshots were at what they did.

Randall dropped the wildland engine into four-wheel low and continued toward the fire until she thought he was going to drive straight into it. She could see Jill in the other engine driving down into the valley ahead of the fire and climbing back up the other side.

The smoke was thicker here. They were close enough that she could see the fire crawling up the trees like a living thing. It crept through the grass beneath the trees, like an orange serpent until it reached the next tree and then raced upward: a flicker and a snap at first, but soon a rush high into the boughs. He drove along the front as if it was no more than a guardrail on the highway. At the end, he turned along the flank, the truck tipping ten degrees sideways due to the grade.

"Here. Take over the wheel." Randall slid

out the uphill-side door and closed it, even though the truck was still idling forward. By the time she slid across, he had fifty feet of one-inch hose pulled off the back and connected to the on-board pump.

"Just roll ahead slow," he spoke calmly over the radio.

"Sheila better not be driving my truck," Candace called back in response from her position on the front line.

Randall shot her a grin and Sheila decided that they'd both ignore her.

Sheila had to flex her hands a few times before she could bring herself to grab onto the steering wheel. Randall walked up to the fire, the flames off the deep grass were as tall as he was. With a casual flick of his wrist, he opened the nozzle and began spraying the fire down.

She was surprised at how easily the flames died. It took her a while to see why. Randall ignored the black area that had already been burned. He concentrated only on the burning line which was truly not very wide. Whenever he reached a tree burning along the line, he'd spray it for an extra moment to kill the fire, but never slowed.

As she became oriented to his world, she learned more of what to watch. In the rear-view mirror, she saw a patch still smoking. She tapped the horn and pointed back when Randall looked at her. He slashed the spray at the smoke, thoroughly inundating it, then continued ahead without breaking stride.

He was so clearly in his element. She appreciated the casual skill with which he and the others of WUI had dealt with everything. But watching him have the same attitude toward an active fire was a real sight to see. He might not be Army, but that didn't stop her from feeling better just for being in his presence.

Over the next hour they traveled a couple of times down to the stream at the bottom of the valley and pumped aboard another five-hundred gallons.

"It's a surreal place. We call it The Black," Randall explained as he rode easily in the passenger seat while she climbed the engine back up the slope through the burned-out char to the fire line. "Part of the natural life cycle in this kind of environment. The grass and the trees know what to do; we're the problem.

There are power lines over that ridge," he pointed one way. "And homes over that one," he pointed the other. "So we have to kill it off even though it's just a baby fire."

"Just a baby?"

"I half think the Captain must have been bored to call us out on this one. Maybe he knew Candace was getting antsy; she's always happiest when she's fighting a fire. Doesn't matter. We'll kill it in plenty of time for dinner."

11

Once they had the flanks doused, Randall drove the truck around to the head, trading with Sheila because he figured he shouldn't flaunt in Candace's face who'd actually been driving all morning.

The crew had been busy and had a long line sliced through the soil. The trench ran twenty feet wide and from his flank, all the way down to the creek, and well up the other side.

"Spray the line behind us," Candace instructed when he pulled up. The look she gave him said that switching drivers hadn't fooled her for a second no matter how hard

Sheila tried to look innocent in the passenger seat.

"Sure," Randall eyed the grassy slope beyond the trench. "Just as soon as you get these amateurs to move their vehicles."

Candace looked over her shoulder and swore. His path was blocked by a tangled array of the volunteer firefighters parked far too close to the line. It only took moments before she had firefighters racing off the line to move their vehicles. Totally overestimating the danger, the volunteers then drove five-hundred yards away. It would take them a while to trudge their way back.

"Better light the backfire soon," he nodded toward the nearly empty line now manned by only a half dozen hotshots along its half-mile length.

The fire head wasn't more than a few hundred feet away and was going to arrive at the line before the stray volunteers did.

A backfire had to be lit right now on the fire-side of the trench they'd cut. Unable to cross the trench, it would slowly burn up the fuels back toward the main fire, robbing it of heat before it hit the line.

"Shit!" Candace got on the radio to the other hotshots and raced off to start the fire.

"Darn it!" Jill's voice came over the radio. She really was too sweet, though with Sheila beside him he was no longer wishing she had a twin sister.

"What?" Candace's voice was harsh, in no mood for additional problems as she sprinted to gather up her own fire torch to ignite the line.

"I'm in the creek," Jill called. "Stuck trying to get back to your side."

Randall looked down the slope and saw the big red engine down in the bottom of the valley. The fire was still running hot through the trees, headed her way. This first fireline was only to get the fire off the slopes. The second battle would be down in the those trees, so there was nothing set up there yet to protect her.

He slammed into gear and raced down the hill toward her, barely remembering to warn Sheila to hang on before he slammed over a foot-thick fallen tree.

"I stuck it good," Jill called out as he drove up. She already had a length of chain hooked up to her front bumper, but the slope was steep and he wouldn't have a lot of extra power to pull her free while trying to climb. Hopefully it would be enough because she was wheel deep in creek water and the fire was on the move.

He backed down as close as he dared, already feeling the first of the fire's heat through the window. Jill shot him a thumbs up as soon as she had the chain hooked up and raced back to her truck.

They eased into first gear together, but it wasn't budging. The fire wasn't going to give him time to unhook, circle around, and try pulling her back the other way.

Sheila cursed from beside him and then was gone with a slam of her door.

He didn't have time to deal with whatever snit-fit she was having. In the rearview mirror he kept an eye on Jill in the stuck fire engine's driver's seat as they tried once more to dislodge it without success.

The warmth of the fire was now up to a hot summer's day and climbing fast. Even with both engines pumping, the flames would be too big to fight directly.

Then, shortly before he was going to call

her to abandon her engine, he saw Sheila stalk up to Jill's driver-side door. She yanked it open and, with little ceremony, shoved Jill over into the passenger seat.

"Give me five feet of slack," her terse command snapped over the radio.

Randall glanced once at the flames. He should call for them to abandon the engine. There would barely be time to undo the chain and get the hell out.

"Don't think. Do it!"

Randall smiled to himself as he eased off the chain. That sounded just like his Sheila.

She began rocking the truck back and forth in the creek. The slick rocks gave her little purchase, but she was getting some motion as she slammed back and forth between drive and reverse.

"On five. Give me everything you've got, Randall."

He shoved in the clutch, shifted into first, and revved the engine. It had better work on five because by ten the fire would overrun both of them.

Sheila counted down her increasing rocking motion.

Her shout of "Now!" came just halfway between a rear swing and a forward one.

Anticipating her, he came off the clutch hard and slammed down on the gas.

The five feet of slack jerked out of the chain, jarring him hard against his seatbelt.

He kept his foot down and the big diesel groaned with power.

As if the creek didn't want to let go, the other engine emerged a foot at a time, sheeting water to the sides.

There was a moment when their momentum hung in the balance as grass and mud sprayed off their spinning tires, but his front pair found some traction on good soil and it was enough to drag them both forward and up the slope.

He checked the rearview and watched as a burning tree crashed down where the engine had been stuck just moments before.

12

"That felt good," Sheila couldn't stop saying it. "That felt soooo good."

"Hey!" Randall complained. "You're only supposed to be saying that about me."

Sheila grabbed Randall and shoved his back against the rear wall of the fire station. He stopped complaining when she kissed him. The joy that coursed through her ran deep and hot and she poured it into the kiss.

His strong arms clamped tight around her just as they had that first night she'd climbed into his bed. Except now it wasn't about being held—it was all about who was holding her.

"You don't feel good, Randall," she nibbled at his neck making him squirm. "You feel incredible!"

He laughed at her crow of delight.

"Will you two cut it out?" Candace stuck her head out the back door of the equipment bay. "We can hear you right through the wall."

"Nope," Sheila had no intention of stopping with Randall any time soon.

Candace looked at her watch. "I figure you have one hour to get home, shower, and get back here after picking up the pies at Sam's place. Get a move on, I don't like my pies or my hotshots to be late." And she slammed the door.

Randall laughed and tried to pull her back into a kiss, but she held off.

Her mental processes really weren't slow. They didn't feel slow anyway. Maybe that was all part of the issue. But she'd heard something that…

"Did Candace just say '*hotshots*'? Plural?"

Randall sobered and turned to study the closed door.

Then she felt his shrug.

"Could be…"

13

The shower was fun as always.

Sheila almost felt shy sharing it with the firefighter that Randall had turned into, but shy had never been a thing between them. Still, now that she knew the hard-core firefighter that lurked beneath his easy-going demeanor, it was like she was with someone else. Someone even better than she'd thought she was with, which was astonishing as she'd been counting herself damned lucky of late.

And Randall got her to smile as they went into the Bavarian Bakery to pick up the pies for dinner; the place was such classic German kitsch. But the sample cinnamon rugelach they'd split had been splendidly authentic.

It was so different walking through town now than it had been a month ago. It didn't matter that the snow was artificial; the town glittered with tiny ice crystals. The polka band was in full swing as were the chaotic crowds of children. She managed to dodge all collisions this time, so there would be no test of their reaction to her—something she still wasn't ready for.

"Damn, I keep forgetting to buy twinkle lights."

He hesitated in front of the Christmas store window, and she didn't even cringe.

"When I told my sister that I was in love, she said I should get some twinkle lights for the bedroom," he set off walking again.

"When you told your sister…*what?*" Sheila ground to a halt. *In love?* Some chattering tourist couple slammed into her from behind and bounced off.

Randall simply smiled at her. "I think making love to you by the light of twinkle lights would be a very good thing."

"No. What's that other thing you said?"

"See? I told you there weren't any issues with your reaction time," he kissed her on the nose and then kept walking toward the fire station with his armful of pie boxes.

Sheila wasn't used to having to scramble to keep up with a man.

Luke came out of a side street not a dozen steps ahead. There were some things that she definitely wasn't going to discuss in front of *him*.

Or at all.

And the crowd built from there.

Or was she?

By the time they reached the fire station, more firefighters and families had joined them. They all greeted her by name, made her feel welcome. Sheila realized that she knew all of their names as well. Had eaten at several of their houses. Knew most of the kids' names too. *When did that happen?*

With no privacy, she could only puzzle at Randall's statement. The problem was that the more she did, the less strange it became. She cared for Randall. She really did. Is that what love felt like? If it was, how in hell was she supposed to know.

It was halfway through the dinner before she was able to track down Candace and ask her what that "hotshots" comment had meant.

"One of the main things I look for when I'm building my hotshot team is what you showed today."

"What's that?"

"You're not afraid of fire. You keep thinking even when it's right on top of you. Damned hard to test that without a real fire."

Sheila had driven through enough shellings and bombardment that the fire hadn't fazed her at all. "What are the other things?"

"Saving my damned engine," Candace grinned at her. "Work with Randall, get your red card. Tryouts are in the spring, not that you need to worry about that." She punched Sheila on the arm like guys did and strutted back into the crowd. It was no longer a surprise that she had married a Navy SEAL and was keeping him happy.

It was only at the end of the night, as she and Randall were walking arm in arm back through the sleeping village that Sheila really connected that this was Christmas Eve…she checked the cuckoo clock in the window of

Der Markt Platz…no, Christmas Day. She'd known it was close. Obligatory call with Mom about whether or not she was coming home for it, etc. etc. But the firehall dinner had just been a Christmas party. Not the official Eve of.

"I didn't get you anything, Randall. Please tell me that you didn't get me a present either."

He looked aside as if seeking a subject change.

"Oh no! What did you get me? Are there any shops open past midnight?" The empty street answered that one. "Maybe McDonald's up on the highway is open and I could get you some French fries."

Now he seemed to be the one having trouble connecting words. After a few slowing paces, he turned and led her away from the shops to the small park where the band had been playing Christmas carols earlier. She could still hear them on the night air. That should have reminded her to get him something, would have if they hadn't been playing them since the moment of her arrival back at Thanksgiving.

He led her to the little gazebo and sat beside her on the bench.

"I got you something," his voice was low and rough. "Probably pretty damned stupid, but…" His shrug showed his sudden unease.

"Just, I don't know, just give it to me and I'll get you something equally stupid when the stores reopen. Then we'll be even." It came out in a mad rush. She didn't know why she was feeling so nervous. It wasn't like her.

"Equally stupid?" There was a tease in his voice that she'd come to like. There was never a hidden agenda behind it; it was more his way of laughing with her rather than at her. And he took her return teases in stride just as easily as he took her silences.

"I promise," Sheila raised her right hand. "Equally stupid."

"Okay," he blew out a hard huff of breath that made a brief cloud in the chill air. He dug into a pocket, pulled out a small box, and opened it.

Inside was a golden ring with a small ruby the color of fire. "It's beautiful. Simple and perfect."

"It's yours, if you want it."

"Of course I do, it's—" and with those words her brain seized up.

I do? Randall hadn't offered her a present. Well, not a present like a present present. Her brain was babbling.

She looked up into his dark eyes and studied him carefully by the soft street lighting. He didn't look away. Didn't shy off.

"You said to just give it to you," he explained. "I had a speech, which I can't remember. I'll kneel if you'd like. But the important part is that every one of my days has been better for having you in it. I'm betting that isn't going to change. I know it won't."

Sheila wanted to protest that she was a wreck, but she didn't feel like one. Not when Randall was around. She felt capable, strong…

She looked at the ring once more. It wasn't as simple as it had first appeared. The band was twisted, like a mobius strip. All one side, the inside becoming the outside and the outside in. It was an elegant piece of work.

And it was who she was, all twisted up, the inside and the outside blurred until they became one because of the man waiting patiently beside her.

Well, not altogether patiently. She knew him well enough to see the strain, but he'd never pushed her to be other than who she was. That's when she knew that the ring wasn't the gift, Randall Jones was. A life-long sized gift.

She leaned forward and kissed him lightly.

"Something equally stupid…" she whispered against his lips. "I promise. I really do."

About the Author

M. L. Buchman has over 50 novels and 30 short stories in print. Military romantic suspense titles from both his Night Stalker and Firehawks series have been named Booklist "Top 10 of the Year," placing two titles on their "Top 101 Romances of the Last 10 Years" list. His Delta Force series opener, *Target Engaged,* was a 2016 RITA nominee. In addition to romance, he also writes thrillers, fantasy, and science fiction.

In among his career as a corporate project manager he has: rebuilt and single-handed a fifty-foot sailboat, both flown and jumped out of airplanes, and designed and built two houses. Somewhere along the way he also bicycled solo around the world.

He is now making his living as a full-time writer on the Oregon Coast with his beloved wife and is constantly amazed at what you can do with a degree in Geophysics. You may keep up with his writing and receive a free 4-novel starter e-library by subscribing to his newsletter at:

www.mlbuchman.com.

Wild Fire (excerpt)
-the riveting conclusion to the Firehawks series-

*"**Gordon. Hit the hotspot** at your two o'clock."*

"*Perfect,*" Gordon Finchley mumbled to himself. The call came from Mark Henderson, the Incident Commander-Air, the moment after Gordon carved his MD 530 helicopter the other way toward a flaming hotspot at eleven o'clock and hit the release on his load of water.

Two hundred gallons spilled down out of his helo's belly tank and punched the cluster of burning alders square in the heart. He glanced back as he continued his turn and the flames were now hidden in the cloud of steam, which meant it was a good hit.

"Die, you dog!" He yelled it at the flames like…Austin Powers…yelling at something. He really had to work on his macho. Or maybe just give it up as a lost cause.

"I have the other one, Mark," Vanessa called up to the ICA from her own MD 530. Her touch of an Italian accent still completely slayed Gordon…and any other guy who met her. Because her "Italian" was more than just her voice.

Gordon twisted his bird enough sideways to watch her, which was always a pleasure, in the air or on the ground. Vanessa Donatella flew her tiny, four-seater helicopter the same way she looked: smooth, beautiful, and just a little bit delicate. Her water attack was also dead on. It punched down the second spot fire, which had been ignited by an ember cast far ahead of the main fire.

The two of them were fighting their aerial battle beyond the head of the wildfire—he and Vanessa were making sure that nothing sparked to life ahead of the line of defense. He could just make out the Mount Hood Aviation smokejumpers suited up in flame-resistant yellow Nomex, defending a ridgeline. The heavy hitters of the main airshow, MHA's three Firehawks and a Twin 212 helicopter, were attacking the primary fire, ducking in and around the columns of smoke and flame to deliver their loads where the smokejumpers most needed them.

He twisted back to straight flight, popped up high enough to clear the leading edge of the flames, then ducked through the thin veil of smoke and dove down over the burning bank at the lake's shore. He could feel the wash of radiated heat through the large windshield that gave him such a great view—a nearly unbroken sweep of acrylic starting below his feet on the rudder pedals, then sweeping above his head. It became much cooler once he punched out over the open lake.

Gordon slid to a hover with his skids just ten feet over the water—low enough to unreel his snorkel hose and let the pump head dip below the lake's surface. It would be forty seconds until he had two hundred more gallons aboard.

Vanessa slid her helo down close beside him and dunked her own hose.

Their helos were identical except for the large identifying numbers on the side. The MD 530 was as small as a helicopter could be and still have four seats. Last season they'd switched from dipping buckets dangling on longlines to belly tanks attached between the skids. There was an art to steering the swinging buckets to their target that Gordon could get nostalgic about, but the tank was certainly more convenient.

Their helos were painted with the MHA colors: gloss black with red-and-orange flames running down the sides. The effect was a bit ruined by the big windshields that made up the whole nose of the aircraft, but Gordon would take the visibility any day.

"Nice hit," he offered. The pilots kept a second radio tuned to a private frequency so that they could coordinate among themselves without interfering with the ICA's commands to the airshow. It also allowed them to chat in these brief quiet moments. In the background was a third radio tuned to the ground team. Thankfully, there weren't any fixed-wing aircraft attacking the fire or there'd be a fourth radio running. When flying solo, it could be harder to fight the radios than the fire.

"You too. It is such a pity that you hit the wrong fire." He could feel Vanessa's warmth in her tease.

"Even a couple seconds more warning would have worked. If I didn't know better, I'd think Mark was doing it on purpose."

"Whine. Whine. Whine."

They shared a smile across the hundred feet that separated them. It was a real bummer that it hadn't worked out between them. After months of silent but—he eventually discovered—mutual attraction, they'd gotten together. Only to have nothing come of it. Making love to someone as beautiful and gentle as Vanessa was a joy, but there'd been no spark. They'd talked about it, tried again, and still nothing. Despite his typical awkwardness around stunning women (most women really) and Vanessa's natural shyness—or perhaps because of the combination—they'd come out of it as close friends. Friends without benefits, which was still a pity, but good friends.

His water tank gauge reached full and he lifted aloft as he reeled in his hose. Vanessa would be about ten seconds behind him.

Together they flew over the flaming bank that sloped steeply up from the lake. No point in fighting that fire, it would burn down to the shore and then there would be nowhere else for it to go. It was simply one flank of the main fire. The head itself was a long burn running south toward a community of homes at the other end of the lake—*that* they had to defend.

Henderson gave him enough lead time to pick his path this time. His whine to Vanessa had some basis. Messing with a pilot didn't sound like Henderson at all, but lately there'd definitely been something going on.

Gordon shrugged to himself.

He was never big on worrying about what came next. After three years of flying for the man, Gordon knew that whatever Henderson's game was, it would show up only when he was good and ready to reveal it. But another part of him—the one that had told his father precisely where he could ram a hot branding iron the day he'd left the family ranch for the last time—decided that if Henderson kept it up, Gordon might need to buy a branding iron of his own.

For now, only the fire mattered. It was getting even more aggressive and it took a punch from both of their birds to kill the next flare-up.

"I'm headed back to base for fuel," Vanessa announced on the command frequency.

"Roger," Henderson called down from his spotter plane three thousand feet above the fire. "Gordon, fly twice as fast."

Typical. "Sure thing, boss man." He flipped a finger aloft, then wiggled his cyclic control side to side to wave at Vanessa by rocking his helicopter. She returned the gesture and peeled off to the northwest. By pure chance, this fire was less than a ten-minute flight from MHA's base on the eastern foothills of Mt. Hood. The eleven-thousand-foot volcanic mountain was a shining beacon of glaringly bright glaciers, even in late September. The midmorning sun was blinding off the high slopes. In moments, Vanessa was a black dot against that white background. She'd be back in under half an hour and then it would be his turn.

Below him was a land of brown and green, heavy on the brown. Eastern Oregon had none of the green lushness that everyone associated with the Oregon Coast and the Willamette Valley. Out here, Ponderosa pine grew far enough apart for grass to grow tall between them. And now, late in the season, the grass was all dried to a dark gold and carried fire fast and hard. The pine and western juniper weren't in much better shape. Several seasons of drought had taken their toll. The hundred-foot grand firs and the fifty-foot alder were all as dry as bone and lit off like Roman candles.

Gordon climbed an extra fifty feet, crossing the worst of it. He remembered back in his rookie year with MHA when Jeannie had a tree blow up directly under her. The superheated sap had cooked off and sent a big chunk of treetop an extra hundred feet aloft. It had knocked out her rear rotor over the New Tillamook Burn Fire. She'd managed to find a clearing the same size as her helo's rotor blades and somehow set down safely in it. Gordon had seen it and still wasn't sure how she'd stuck that landing.

He kept up the hustle: lake, climb over fire, hit the latest flare-up, climb back over, and dive down for more water. Occasionally one of the big helos would be tanking at the same moment he was. He'd always liked his little MD. The Firehawks—the firefighting version of the Black Hawk helicopters—could carry a thousand gallons to his two hundred, and they were damn fast in flight, but they had none of the finesse of his MD. They didn't get up close and personal with the fire. They flew higher and could knock crown fires out of trees. He flew lower and could put out your campfire without messing up the rest of the campsite… well, not too much.

He harassed his best friend Mickey at one point in his Twin 212 as they tankered together. Two-twelves were midsized helos, halfway between his own MD and the big Firehawks— the modern version of the Vietnam-era UH-1 Hueys. It made for a good spread of capabilities on the team, but it didn't mean he had to let Mickey fly easy just because of that.

"Hey buddy, you actually getting any work done?"

"More than you, Finchley."

"Believe that when I see it. Honeymoon over yet?"

"Not even close!" Mickey sounded pretty damned pleased.

"You better be saying that, hubbie" Robin cut in as she hovered her big Firehawk *Oh-one* down over the water.

Gordon was glad for Mickey. His easygoing friend had fallen for Robin, the brash, hard-edged blonde, the moment she'd hit camp at the beginning of the year. They were an unlikely couple from the outside, but it looked like it was working for them. They'd hooked up on day one, married last month, and showed no signs of the heat easing—of course, anything involving Robin Harrow would be fiery hot. Gordon wasn't jealous, he really wasn't. MHA's lead pilot was a primal force and would have run right over any lesser man than Mickey. Way too out there for Gordon. The quiet Vanessa had seemed about perfect for him, except instead of fire between them, there hadn't even been ignition.

Not being jealous was one thing. But when they were in camp during those rare quiet moments of the busy fire season, Mickey paid much more attention to Robin than to his old still-single pal. Gordon supposed it only made sense, but he was all the happier about finding a friend in Vanessa to fill that unexpected void.

Up over the fire, they headed for their respective targets.

The real battle, the make-or-break on the fire, was going to happen in the next thirty minutes. Gordon checked his fuel. Yes, he'd be good for that long and Vanessa would be back in another ten.

The wildfire would soon be slamming up against the fire break that the smokies had punched through the trees. Flames were climbing two hundred feet into the air in a thick pall of smoke gone dark gray with all of the ash that the heat was carrying aloft.

With a single load, Gordon managed to hit three separate flare-ups behind the smokies' line. He could see the soot-stained smokie team below, clearing brush and scraping soil by hand even though the main flames were less than a hundred feet away. They had inch-and-a-half hoses charged up and were spraying down their own line.

Gordon swung for the lake, climbed through the smoke, and dove—

Something slammed into his windshield straight in front of his face.

He flinched and jerked.

Wrong shape and color for a bird.

Mechanical!

A hobby drone. A big one. Four rotors and a camera.

It star-cracked his acrylic windshield, then slid upward.

He didn't have a moment to plead with the fates before he felt his MD jolt.

Perfect—the drone slid straight into his engine's air intake.

Not a chance that his Allison 250 turboshaft engine would just chew up the plastic and spit it out the exhaust. Even if it did, the battery was like throwing a brick into the turbine.

The primary compressor, spinning at fifty thousand RPM, choked on the three-pound drone.

A horrendous grinding noise sounded close above his head.

Red lights flared, starting with "Engine Out" at the upper left of his console and a high warning tone in his headset.

Other indicators flared to life, but he ignored them. With the engine failed, nothing else really mattered.

Gordon eased down on the collective and twisted the throttle to the fuel cutoff position. The grinding sound slowed but grew rapidly worse—his engine wasn't just dead, it was shredding itself. He slammed a foot on the right pedal as the nose torqued to the left.

"Mayday! Mayday! Mayday!" At least he still had electrical power to the radios. "Hobby drone strike, straight into my engine. Going down."

The radio fired up with questions, but Gordon was in the death zone and didn't have time to listen. A lift-failure emergency in a helicopter below fifty feet or over four hundred was generally survivable. The range in between those two altitudes cut life expectancy a lot more than he wanted to think about at the moment. He was currently in heavy smoke, descending down through the one-fifty mark.

It was little comfort knowing that the FAA would slap the drone owner's wrist if they could find him. Of course, if this went as badly as Gordon was expecting, MHA would go after the asshole for a million-dollar helo and the cost of one funeral.

"God damn it! And I was in such a good mood." There, that sounded more like Vin Diesel than Austin Powers. Truly sad—he was going to have to die to get it right. Though he couldn't place what movie the line was from.

The smoke wrapped around him and visibility left altogether. He fought for best auto-rotate speed, but at the rate he was falling, there wasn't a whole lot of time to get there.

He'd started flying fifteen years ago on his family's ranch, spent the last three years with MHA, and this was his first real-life crash landing. All the practice in the world didn't count for shit.

His palms were sweating against the slick plastic of the controls. The cabin was filling with smoke, but he couldn't take his hands off the controls to close the vent to the outside.

With his right shoulder, he nudged up the

release lever on the pilot-side door. It swung open two inches and stabilized just like it was supposed to. The additional airflow helped the smoke flow through the cabin faster, but it still burnt his eyes and his throat. As a firefighter, he supposed that it was no surprise that death smelled like hot wood smoke.

His visibility was under twenty feet, and the smoke was taking on a distinctly orange glow. At sixty miles an hour, that gave him absolutely no lead time for maneuvering.

He wrestled east for the water.

The first treetop that slapped against his windshield was brilliant orange with flame. Lodgepole pine.

The next one, Douglas fir, snagged his left skid, jerking him sharply to the side before he was past it. If the one that slammed into his right-side pilot's window, white fir, made him scream, he didn't have time to realize it.

The next one, too buried in flames to recognize, ripped the door off entirely.

Gordon's instincts did what they could, with the controls now gone useless. One tree after another battered his helo: Ponderosa, western juniper—he ricocheted off the side of a massive Doug fir harder than being tossed by a bucking bronc.

The ends of rotor blades snapped off.

Then more of them.

The other skid snagged and twisted him the other direction, which saved him from the next flaming tree coming in through the missing door and killing him.

He realized that he was falling, treetop to treetop, down the steep bank toward the water.

His broken helicopter smashed through the last of the flaming line in a slow tumble thirty feet above the water.

With one final effort, he stomped on the right pedal and shoved the cyclic left.

No rotors. No effect.

That's when he remembered where the movie line was from. It wasn't Vin Diesel at all. It was John Goodman playing the hapless Al Yackey in the firefighting movie *Always*.

"No offense, John," he spoke his final words aloud to his dead helicopter. "But I'd rather die as Vin Diesel."

He plunged into the water upside down.

* * *

Five minutes earlier, Ripley Vaughan flew into sight of the firefight and eased her Erickson Aircrane to a hover.

"Wow!" "That's a mess!" Brad and Janet White, her married copilot and crew chief, did one of their synchro-speaking things.

They were right. It was.

The Black, the area already burned by the wildfire, ranged across five hundred acres. No cleanup had been done, there were spot fires dotted all over the Black, and the fire's flanks were eating sideways into the trees in addition to the main head of the fire driving toward a community. It could be the textbook definition of zero percent contained.

Ripley could see the hard slash of a smokejumper defense line across the rugged hills, cleared of trees and brush. It looked so small against the towering wall of fire bearing down on them, but then it always did from altitude. And there was a heavy airshow going on. The battle of this wildfire was about to be engaged big time.

They needed help. But without a contract, she wouldn't be insured *or* paid if she fought on this fire…unless.

"Are those aircraft painted black?"

Brad pulled out a small pair of binoculars. "Yep! With flames and all."

That meant it was Mount Hood Aviation, their new outfit.

Ripley watched the airshow for another thirty seconds and could see the smooth coordination of the attack effort. She'd been flying her big Aircrane helicopter to fire for a couple of years, but had never imagined she'd get the chance to fly for Mount Hood Aviation. They had the best reputation in the business. Their for-hire smokejumping team was right on par with the Forest Service's Missoula, Montana Zulies, but *nobody* had the renown of their helicopter team.

Back at Erickson's Medford airfield in southern Oregon, Randy had called her into his office.

"I've got a rest-of-season contract request here."

Ripley hadn't particularly cared where she went, as long as it kept her flying.

"For some reason, it came through with your name on it. Something going on here I don't know about?" He sounded some kinda pissed about it. Upsetting a chief pilot with his years of experience was never a good idea—especially not when he signed her paychecks. Randy's cheerful demeanor and the easy smile that normally showed through his white beard were completely missing. Now she could see a flash of that kick-ass retired Army Chief Warrant that was typically hidden away. Word was that he'd graduated top of his Army flight class and hadn't slowed down for an instant during his years with the 2/10 Air Cav, not that the stories ever came from him.

"Unless it's for dancing," Ripley eyed the paperwork Randy was waving at her, "I can't imagine why it would be for me."

With her crew being named Brad and Janet—and Janet looking like a young Susan Sarandon, it was inevitable that their crew would learn "The Time Warp" dance from *The Rocky Horror Picture Show*…and then get known for it. But she hadn't been shopping for someplace else to be; she liked flying for Erickson more than she had liked anything else since she'd left the Navy.

Randy had tossed over the paperwork and Ripley had glanced down at it. She didn't spot her name anywhere. It was a contract for "your best pilot" from Mount Hood Aviation.

His scowl changed to his usual cheery smile. "Man's gotta have some fun. A couple pilots here are as good as you, but I don't have any that are better. You want to fly with MHA for what's left of the season, it's yours. You've earned it. But…" and he'd aimed a finger out toward the landing apron where her helicopter baked under the Medford late-summer heat. That former-military voice came out again, "You better bring my bird back in one piece. Yourself too, while you're at it."

She'd promised she would and then signed it on the spot. It was only later that she thought to ask Brad and Janet, but they were game as always.

The three of them with their Aircrane were supposed to be transiting to MHA's base today but now had stumbled on their new outfit in a full-on firefight.

"Janet, let's scoop up some water. Brad, find me this fire's Air Attack frequency because I can't fly into a restricted Fire Traffic Area without permission."

There was a lake down below that she

could see the other helos were using. It was just long enough that she could use the sea snorkel instead of the pond snorkel. The latter would require hovering and pumping. The sea snorkel was designed to let her fill her tanks on the fly. She could lower the snorkel's long strut to drag the tip below the surface and use the force of her own flying speed to fill the tanks. It was much quicker.

She flew down over the south end of Rock Creek Reservoir.

"Snorkel in five," she called out. Ripley could run the controls from her left side command seat, but since she had her crew chief aboard for the transit, Ripley let her have something to do. Her real duties would be on the ground once they arrived, but it was a chance for Janet to get a little control time in her log book.

"In five," Janet called back. She sat in the observer's seat directly behind Ripley, facing backward. That seat was positioned so that a pilot could control the helo during finicky winching jobs, like when they were assembling transmission towers. Not really needed for firefighting, but it gave her crew chief somewhere to sit and be a part of the firefight.

Ripley flew down until her big helo's wheels were just ten feet above the water. Once they slowed to thirty knots, Janet lowered the sea snorkel's strut into the water. Their speed alone would cause the water to shoot into the two submerged openings on the pipe, each the size of her palm. The water would blow upward like a thirty-five-mile-an-hour firehose. In forty seconds and just over half a mile, they could load up twenty-five hundred gallons of water, a dozen large hot tubs' worth, and be heading for the fire.

She flew along the line of the burning shore as it curved around from east to north. Rock Creek entered at the northern tip of the reservoir, providing her with an excellent gap in the trees for her climb out.

Brad found the frequency.

MHA's communications blasted into Ripley's headset.

"Did anyone see where he went down?" The voice was nearly frantic.

"All aircraft," a powerful male voice called out over the airwaves. "Climb and pull back. There was a civilian drone over the fire. It's already taken out one of our birds, we don't want to lose another. We need to evacuate. Keep an eye out for Gordon, but continue retreat."

Ripley had been on a number of fires where all of the air attack—helicopters, fixed-wing tankers, and command aircraft—had to pull back because someone had spotted a stupid civilian drone. There wasn't a firefighter aloft who hadn't thought about the dangers. But…

Ripley pressed the button on the back of the cyclic control with the tip of her index finger and transmitted. "If it already hit someone, then it's out of the sky. The chances of two simultaneous idiots on the same fire seems pretty low."

"Identify!" The ICA snapped out the command.

"This is Erickson Aircrane *Diana*—Oh shit!"

Ripley saw the body floating directly in her path. It was too late to avoid by climbing or raising the sea snorkel's strut.

* * *

Gordon had been floating on his back, watching the sky. It was amazing how pretty the sky was when you'd suddenly been given a reprieve from certain death. Even the fire still raging along the shore was a wonder of smoke and light as it swirled aloft.

He wanted to feel sad about the loss of his helo, but it was hard. His MD 530 had seen him through hell and given its own life to save his. He'd managed to release his seat harness and swim free before the helo hit the bottom of the reservoir. That first breath of air had been so clear and so sharp that he'd never forget it, not for as long as he lived.

A low thrumming echoed through the water, a heavy bass beat that only a helicopter could create, a big one like a Firehawk.

He opened his eyes and lifted his head to see if they'd come for him.

From less than a hundred feet away, he looked straight into the face of a beautiful helicopter pilot.

If there were moments he was never going to forget, the next three seconds were clogged with them.

The pilot sat almost fully exposed by the curved windshield of the helicopter. Gorgeous. Her straight black hair fell past her shoulders.

Her skin was the color of mid-roast coffee with just that perfect amount of cream. Her dark glasses and pilot's helmet with mic boom added to the image. Hot professional female pilot.

The next impression was how huge the approaching helicopter was—and because it was so close, it seemed twice its normal size. Instead of the vicious sleekness of a Black Hawk, it had a bulbous nose and was brilliant orange like the Muppet Beaker, who always looked as alarmed as Gordon was starting to feel.

The last impression, more memorable than anything else—except perhaps that knock-out pilot now looking almost directly down at him—was the long white boom that the Aircrane was slicing through the water.

Straight toward him!

There wasn't time to react. Hell, there wasn't even time to blink.

Gordon braced himself to be chopped in two.

Available at fine retailers everywhere.

Other works by M.L. Buchman

Flash of Fire
Wild Fire

Smokejumpers
Wildfire at Dawn
Wildfire at Larch Creek
Wildfire on the Skagit

Delta Force
Target Engaged
Heart Strike

Angelo's Hearth
Where Dreams are Born
Where Dreams Reside
Maria's Christmas Table
Where Dreams Unfold
Where Dreams Are Written

Eagle Cove
Return to Eagle Cove
Recipe for Eagle Cove
Longing for Eagle Cove
Keepsake for Eagle Cove

Deities Anonymous
Cookbook from Hell: Reheated
Saviors 101

Dead Chef Thrillers
Swap Out!
One Chef!
Two Chef!

SF/F Titles

Nara
Monk's Maze
The Me and Elsie Chronicles

Newsletter signup at:
www.mlbuchman.com

20636873R00059

Printed in Great Britain
by Amazon